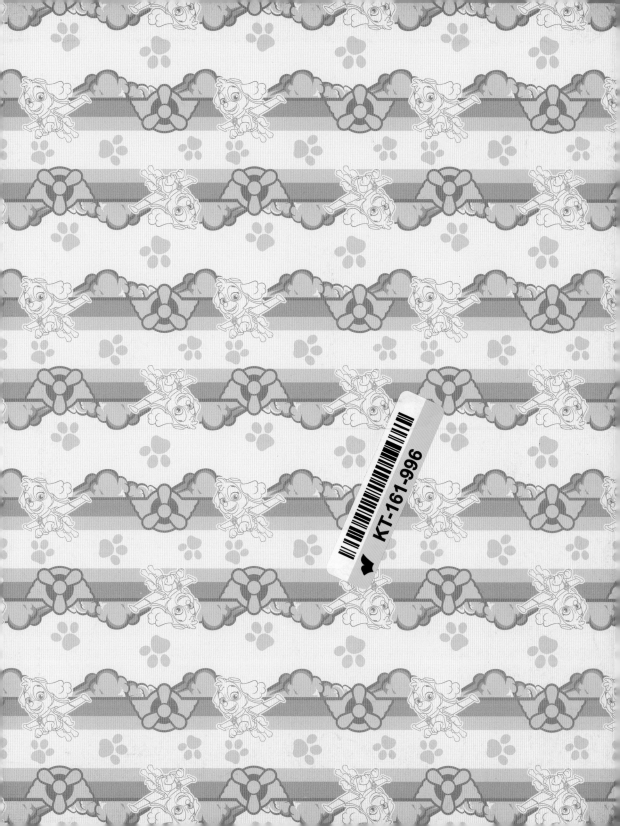

KT-161-996

This edition published by Parragon Books Ltd in 2017

Parragon Books Ltd
Chartist House
15–17 Trim Street
Bath BA1 1HA, UK
www.parragon.com

ISBN 978-1-4748-7644-5

Printed in China

Skye-high Rescue

Bath • New York • Cologne • Melbourne • Delhi
Hong Kong • Shenzhen • Singapore

Skye can't wait for her hero, the talented stunt pilot Ace Soarensen, to arrive in Adventure Bay. Ace is going to perform her daring air show.

Skye races over to Zuma, Rocky and Marshall to share the news.

"We'll get to watch Ace do her amazing tricks in person!" Skye says. The pups are excited.

Just then, Ryder receives a worrying call from Ace.

"Hi, Ace," Ryder says. "I can't wait to see your air show!"

"About that ..." Ace replies. "Seems my plane's having some engine trouble. I'm going to try to make it to Adventure Bay, but it's getting dark and I need a safe place to land."

"Don't worry, Ace, the PAW Patrol is on it!" he tells her. "No job is too big, no pup is too small."

Ryder uses his PupPad to call the PAW Patrol to the Lookout.

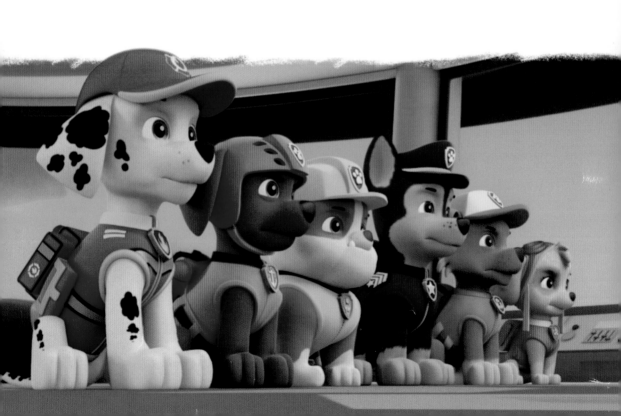

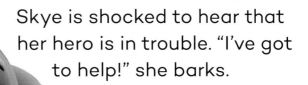

Skye is shocked to hear that her hero is in trouble. "I've got to help!" she barks.

"Of course, Skye," replies Ryder. "I need you to use your helicopter and night-vision goggles to help Ace land safely in the big field at Farmer Yumi's."

"Chase, I need you to use your cones to set up a runway in Farmer Yumi's field and use your light to guide Ace there," Ryder tells him.

"And Rocky," Ryder says, "when the plane lands, I'll need you to help Ace with repairs straight away."

The PAW Patrol is on a roll!

Ryder uses the PupPad on his bike to locate Ace. They find her flying round Jake's Mountain with smoke streaming from her plane.

Skye catches up with Ace and begins to guide her towards a safe landing. But suddenly sparks fly out from the wings of Ace's plane!

"It looks like my luck is running out," Ace says.

Ryder pops up
on her screen.
"Don't worry,
Ace," he says.
"Just follow Skye.
Chase is going to set
up a landing strip in
Farmer Yumi's field."

"I'll take the lead, Ace,"
Skye says. She flies out in
front and heads towards Farmer Yumi's field.

At the field, Chase sets up the cones to mark out a runway but Ryder soon spots a problem. The runway is too dark to see from the air!

"I'm on it," barks Chase. He opens his Pup Pack and shines his flashlight up into the sky.

"Great work," says Ryder, "but your light only shows them where we are. We need to light up the whole runway."

Ryder has an idea. "Rocky, do you have any old torches in your truck?"

"Sure, I've got loads," Rocky says. He tapes the torches to each cone along the runway.

Ryder calls Skye. "You should be near the farm now, Skye. Look for the runway lights."

"Roger that," Skye replies. She soon spots the lights. "Almost there," she calls to Ace.

Suddenly, a loud popping sound comes from Ace's plane and the engine cuts out!

"Oh no, the plane's going down fast!" Ace cries. "I've got to jump...."

Skye calls Ryder to tell him. "Ace has to parachute out!"

"In the dark? But she won't be able to see where she's landing," Ryder says. He thinks for a moment. "I know ... Ace, have you ever done any wing-walking?"

"It's my favourite stunt!" Ace says.

"Great!" says Ryder. "Skye, drop your harness from the helicopter. If Ace can get out on the wing and attach it to herself, she won't have to parachute."

"Roger, Ryder!" calls Skye. "You copy, Ace?"

"Meet you on the wing," Ace replies.

Skye drops the harness from her helicopter and flies closer to Ace's plane.

Ace jumps for the harness, but she misses it. "Sorry, Skye," she says, "not sure I can grab it. I've got my parachute on. I'm going to jump!"

Skye won't let Ace give up. "We can do this, Ace," she says. "I'll get as close as I can."

Carefully, Skye flies her helicopter down even lower. Ace reaches for the harness and grabs it. "I've got her!" Skye says.

"Great, Skye," Ryder says. "We're waiting for you both at Yumi's farm."

Now that she's safe, Ace asks Ryder to check on her plane, Amelia.

"No problem," says Ryder. "I can track Amelia from right here." Ryder pulls up the map and tracks the plane to the bay.

"Ace's plane is heading for a water landing," Ryder reports. "Chase, let's head to the bay and try to get it onto the beach before it sinks."

"Chase is on the case!" barks Chase.

Then Ryder calls Marshall on the PupPad. "Marshall, we need you to do a medical check on Ace to make sure she's okay."

Marshall nods. "I'm on my way!"

Meanwhile, Rocky is waiting for Skye and Ace as they land safely on the ground.

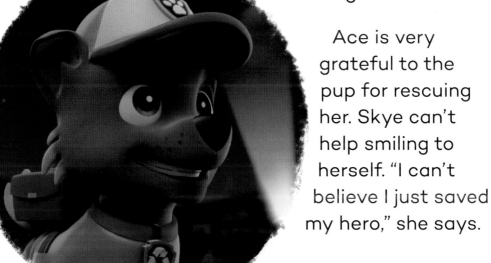

Ace is very grateful to the pup for rescuing her. Skye can't help smiling to herself. "I can't believe I just saved my hero," she says.

Rocky and Marshall race over to them. Using his X-ray screen, Marshall checks to make sure Ace hasn't broken any bones.

Marshall gives her the all-clear and then they race off to check on Ace's plane.

When they get there, Ace is pleased to find the PAW Patrol has saved Amelia! "I don't think she'll be ready for an air show tomorrow," Ace says, looking at the damage.

"Don't worry, Ace," says Ryder. "Whenever you're in trouble, just yelp for help!"

Ace and the pups fix Amelia together, and soon she's as good as new. "I couldn't have done it without the PAW Patrol!" she says.

"I can't wait for the air show tomorrow," says Skye.

"Skye," says Ace, "I know how you can see my tricks up close...."

The next day, the pups line up to watch Ace's amazing air show. As she climbs out onto the wing of her plane they see ... Skye in the pilot seat!

"Look, it's Skye!" cries Rubble. "She's so good!"

Ryder smiles proudly at the PAW Patrol. "You're all good pups!"